JellyTelly Press is a division of JellyTelly, LLC.

FaithWords is a division of Hachette Book Group, Inc. The FaithWords name and logo are trademarks of Hachette Book Group, Inc.

FaithWords
Hachette Book Group
1290 Avenue of the Americas, New York, NY 10104

hachettebookgroup.com | faithwords.com | jellytelly.com

Buck Denver and Friends created by Phil Vischer. *Buck Denver Asks®.. What's in the Bible?* trademark and character rights are owned by Phil Vischer IP, LLC and used by permission under license from Jellyfish One, LLC.

Written by Phil Vischer
Illustrated by Greg Hardin and Kenny Yamada

Art Direction and Design: John Trent
Creative Direction: Phil Vischer and Anne Fogerty

First Edition: February 2019

Library of Congress Cataloging-in-Publication Data has been applied for.
10 9 8 7 6 5 4 3 2 1
ISBN: 978-1-5460-1188-0
Printed in China
APS

Buck Denver's
BAD, Bad Day
A Lesson in THANKFULNESS

Written by Phil Vischer
Illustrated by Greg Hardin & Kenny Yamada

Sunday School Lady and Marcy were setting up for a big party at church.

It was going to be great, with food and games and even a piñata to hit with a stick.

Suddenly they heard a loud scream outside the church!

Marcy didn't believe monsters were real, but she ran outside anyway to see what was going on.

"Goodness gracious!" said Sunday School Lady, pointing at something on the playground. "What's THAT?"

THAT was a person who looked sort of like Buck Denver,
but with a GIANT HEAD. A giant Buck Denver head!
A giant, grinning, big-eyed Buck Denver head!

"I'm not a monster!" said the big-eyed Buck Denver head.

People were running in all directions to get away.

"Calm down, everyone!" yelled Sunday School Lady.
"It's not a monster—it's a person in a costume."

Marcy bravely walked up to the big-eyed Buck Denver.

"Who's in there?" she asked. "Why are you dressed as Buck Denver?"

"I AM Buck Denver!" the voice replied.

Marcy tried again. "Well, you LOOK like Buck Denver! And you DRESS like Buck Denver! And you even SOUND like Buck Denver!"

Sunday School Lady looked closely at the giant head. "I think it IS Buck Denver. He's wearing some sort of a mask ... a crazy-happy sorta scary mask."

"Yes!" said the giant head. "I'm wearing my happy mask!"

"Buck," Marcy asked, "why do you need a happy mask?"

The real Buck Denver slumped to the ground.

"Because I'm having a bad, bad day," he said.

Buck told them about his day. He couldn't find his toothbrush.
He burned his toast. He spilled strawberry jelly on his favorite blue tie.
And that was all before he even left the house!

"Oh, Buck, I'm sorry," said Sunday School Lady. "It's no fun having a bad, bad day. But wearing a happy mask on the outside isn't going to make you happy on the inside."

Marcy lifted up Buck's mask.
Yep. Buck looked miserable.

"So what do I do on a bad, bad day?
I feel MISERABLE!" Buck said.

Sunday School Lady smiled at Buck. "The answer doesn't come from outside, it comes from inside. The answer, Buck, is **THANKFULNESS.**"

Buck was confused.

"Thankfulness? What do I have to be thankful for? Didn't you hear about my bad, bad day?"

Sunday School Lady thought hard.

"I know what you need. You need to hear a couple of stories," she said. "The first one is about Jehoshaphat."

"Jehosha-WHAT?" Buck replied.

"Not Jehosha-WHAT, Jehosha-PHAT!"

Sunday School Lady got out her flannelgraph. It wasn't an ordinary flannelgraph, though. It was a MAGIC flannelgraph.

"Hi, Magic Flannelgraph! Take us to Jehoshaphat!"

She tapped it three times with her pointer and BOOM!

Suddenly Buck wasn't looking AT the flannelgraph,
he was IN the flannelgraph!

"It's fuzzy in here," he said. "Like a PEACH!"

Sunday School Lady smiled. They were standing in a field in Israel, thousands of years ago. In the distance a huge army was preparing for battle.

"Who's THAT guy?" Buck asked. "He looks like a KING!"

"That's Jehoshaphat!" Sunday School Lady answered.
"And he is having a BAD, BAD DAY!"

"Did he burn his toast?" Marcy wondered.

"No—way worse. Jehoshaphat was Israel's king when Israel wasn't very strong, and they were in BIG trouble. THREE different nations had joined their armies together and were coming to DESTROY Israel! They didn't stand a chance!"

"Whoa," Buck said. "That's a really bad day!"

"Even worse than losing your toothbrush!" Marcy added.

Buck agreed. "So what did he do? Did he run away and hide?"

"This is the wild part," Sunday School Lady continued.

"Jehoshaphat and the people of Israel prayed to God and asked for His help. They asked to be saved. But then they did something REALLY weird. They THANKED God."

"For what?" Buck asked. "He hadn't saved them yet!"

"No," said Sunday School Lady. "They thanked God for LOVING them. They thanked God for being who He is!"

"And then, as they were giving thanks and singing, God turned the three nations against each other! Instead of fighting Israel, they started fighting each other and Israel was saved!"

"That's amazing!"
said Buck. "I THINK
I understand ..."

"How about another story just to be sure ... let's see ..."
Sunday School Lady had an idea. She tapped the
ground three times and said, "Brother Louie!"

And BOOM! Brother Louie was in the flannelgraph!

"Hey!" he said. "It's really fuzzy in here!
Like my favorite corduroy pants."

"No time for that, Brother Louie. We need you to tell us a story."
Sunday School Lady tapped the ground again.

Brother Louie looked around.

"Ah yes—I know where we are. Jerusalem!"
he said. "Do you know who THAT is?"

Buck and Marcy saw a familiar face coming over the hill.

"That's Jesus!" Marcy yelled. "But He looks really sad."

"Is HE having a bad, bad day too?" Buck asked.

"Yes, He is," Brother Louie continued.

"Jesus is visiting a very good friend. He should be happy except He knows something is wrong. His good friend has died."

"Oh, that's sad," Marcy said.

"It is. His friend's name is Lazarus. Jesus knows how sad Lazarus' family is and seeing them at the cave where Lazarus is buried makes Jesus sad too. Seeing them cry makes Jesus cry too."

Then they saw Jesus do something a little unusual. He thanked God.

Buck was confused. "Why did Jesus thank God? For NOT saving Lazarus?"

"No," Brother Louie explained. "He thanked Him for being God. Jesus thanked God for being His always-loving, always-powerful Heavenly Father even on bad, bad days.

And then Jesus said, 'Lazarus, come out of there!' And Lazarus got up and walked right out of the cave! He was alive again!"

"Wow!" Buck yelled. Then he thought really, really hard. "So ... if I thank God, does that mean God will do whatever I want? He'll fix everything for me right away?"

Sunday School Lady smiled. "No, Buck. God won't do whatever YOU want. God does whatever HE wants. Because He's God!"

Brother Louie chimed in. "We don't only thank God for giving us what we want. We also thank God for being who He is. All good. All loving. All powerful. All the time. Jesus and Jehoshaphat knew that God is all those things—even on bad, bad days!"

"And THAT'S worth thanking Him for!" Buck said with a big grin.

"There's that smile again!" Sunday School Lady said as she tapped the ground with her pointer.

And BOOM! They were back at the church.

Marcy was excited. "So we can thank God on bad, bad days—not because He's going to do what WE want, but because He's going to do what HE wants."

"AND because of who He is," Buck added. "All good! All loving! All powerful! All the time!"

Brother Louie noticed Buck's mask on the ground and pointed at it.

"Oh, yeah," Buck said. "Guess I won't need that anymore."

"Sure you don't want to keep it, Buck?" asked Sunday School Lady.

"I can't see anything when I wear it!" Buck answered. "What's it good for?"

Suddenly Marcy had an idea.

"I think I know!"

Family Connection

Help your family **KNOW** the love of God,
GROW in God's love, and **SHOW** God's love to others.

CONNECT after reading:

ASK:

1. Why was Buck Denver having a bad, bad day? Have you ever had a bad day? What happened?
2. What did Jehoshaphat do when he was having a bad day?
3. Why do you think Jesus thanked God even though He was sad about His friend Lazarus?
4. What good things can you thank God for when you are having a bad day?
5. How can knowing God is always good, all of the time change the way we respond when we have a bad, bad day?

READ:

- Read more about Jehoshaphat's thankfulness in 2 Chronicles 20.
- Read the story of Lazarus in John 11:1-44.

REMEMBER:

God is good and worthy of our thanks every day—no matter what!

"Give thanks in all circumstances; for this is the will of God in Christ Jesus for you."
1 Thessalonians 5:18

For more family fun, check out jellytelly.com, a partner for Christian parents.